RAYMOND BRIGGS

The Complete Father Christmas

Comprising 'Father Christmas' & 'Father Christmas Goes on Holiday'

PUFFIN BOOKS

D1263807

Father Christmas

For my Mother and Father

Father Christmas

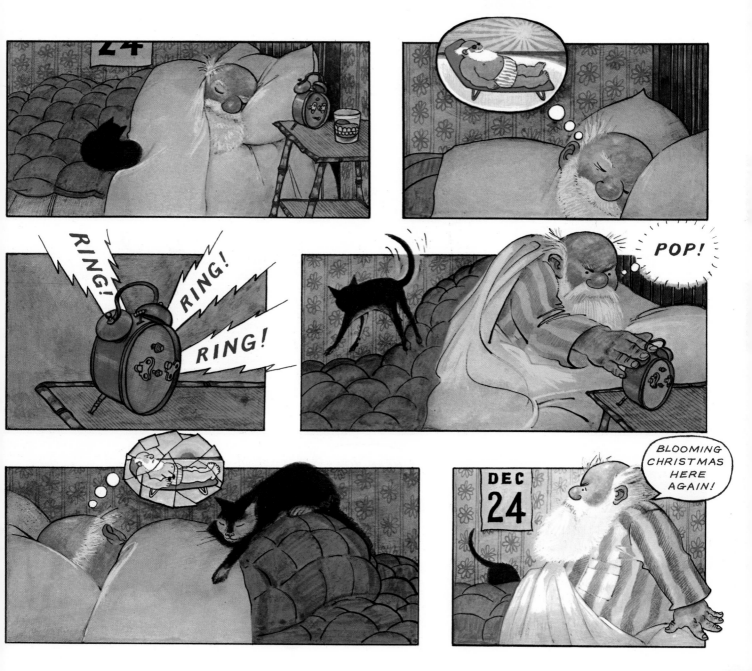

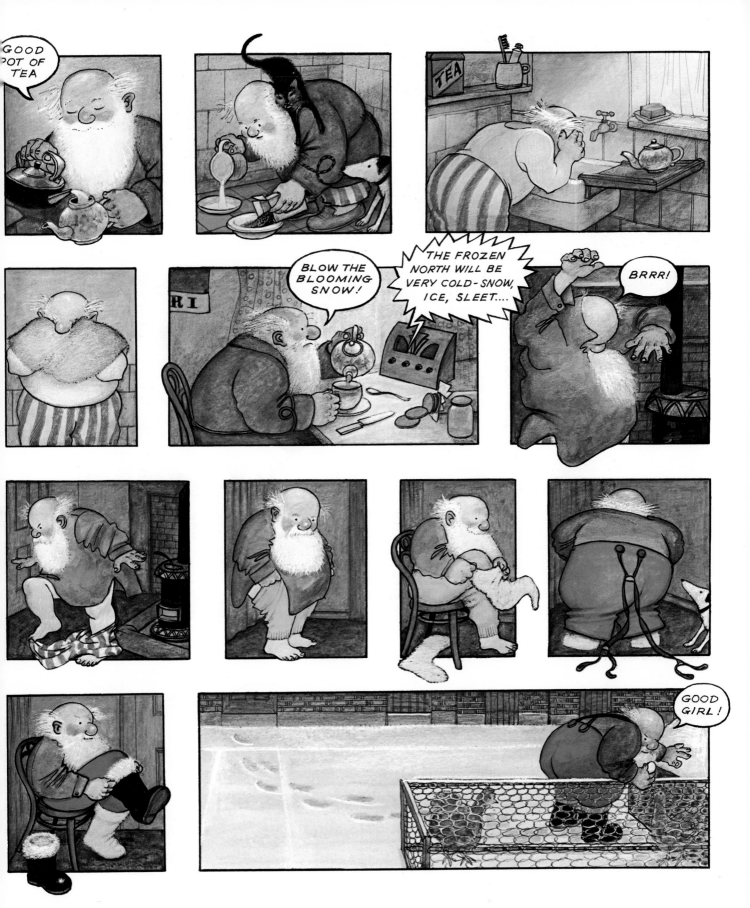

ROLL ON SUMMER!

BRR! BLOOMING COLD!

WORK, WORK, WORK!

GOODBYE CAT

GOODBYE DOG

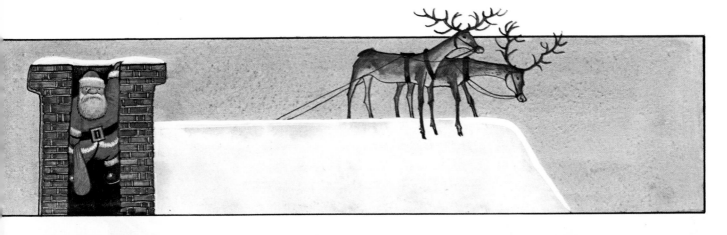

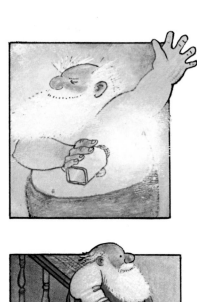

NICE CLEAN SOCKS

GOOD DROP OF ALE.

LOVELY GRUB!

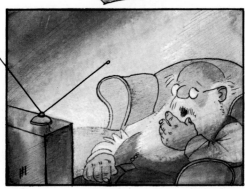

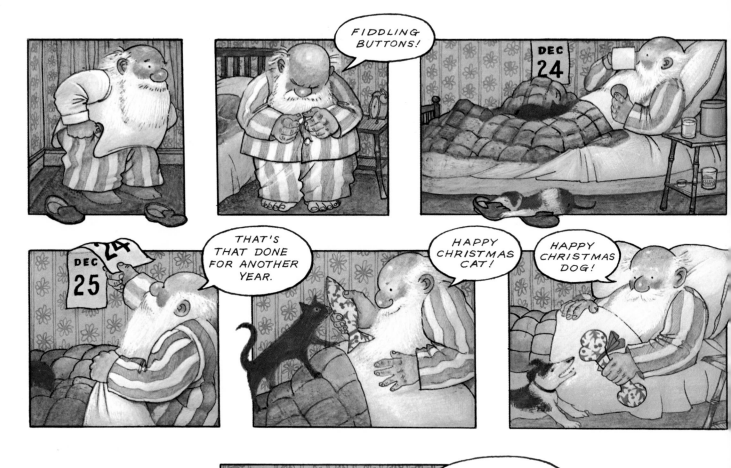

The End

Father Christmas
Goes on Holiday

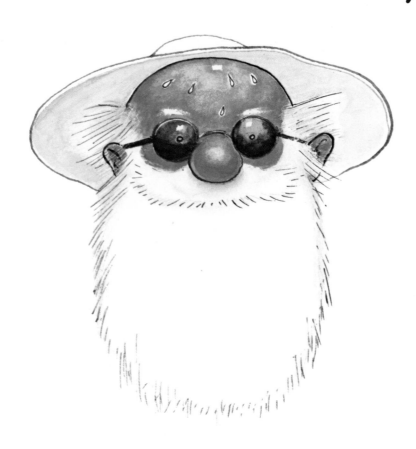

For Jean

Father Christmas Goes on Holiday

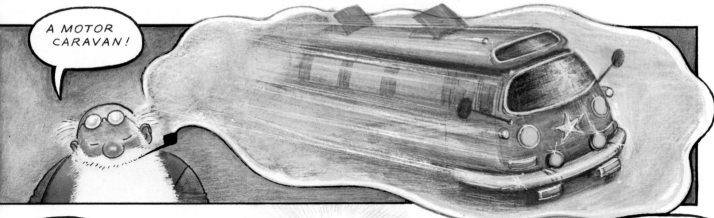

LA BELLE FRANCE!

-ER, BONJOUR, MADEMOISELLE

MADAME! S'IL VOUS PLAIT! BONJOUR, M'SIEUR

OH — ER, PARDON, **MADAME** - ER - JE VEUX ACHETER LE LAIT, S'IL VOUS PLAIT

DU LAIT? OUI, M'SIEUR

MERCI, MADAME!

MERCI, M'SIEUR!

I SPOKE FRENCH! I SPOKE FRENCH!

THIS IS THE LIFE!

WHAT'S THAT?

BLOOMING MARVELLOUS!

GOLDEN ORIOLE! NEVER SEEN ONE BEFORE. ONE MORE TO TICK OFF

BETTER GO HOPPING IN A MINUTE

BLOOMING FUNNY BREAD

WISH I DIDN'T LOOK SO LIKE A BLOOMING FOREIGNER

AH!

BLEU DE TRAVAIL

MAGNIFIQUE, M'SIEUR!

THAT'S BETTER— LOOK MORE FRENCH, NOW

NOT SO CONSPICUOUS

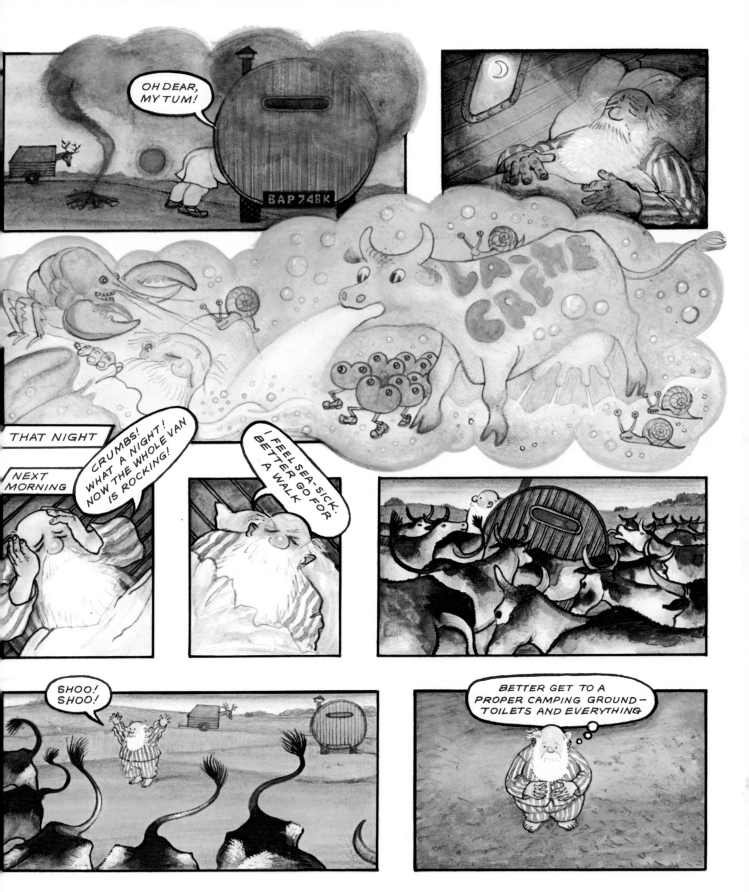

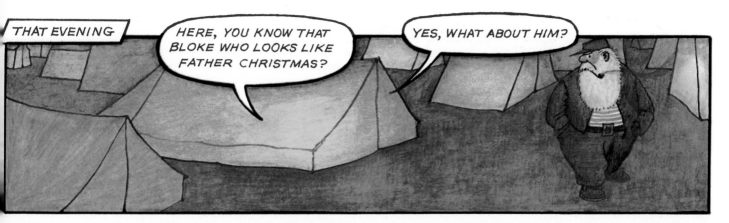

NEXT DAY

CRUMBS! WHAT A PLACE!

WELL, AT LEAST THERE'S PLENTY OF PURE WATER

WHAT'S THAT?

HERON! BLOOMING MARVELLOUS!

BETTER GET THE SHOPPING

JOLLY COLD!

AAAARGH!

GOOD MORNING

QUICK! LOCK THE DOOR!

RAIN ~ COLD SHARKS! WHAT A COUNTRY!

BETTER GET OUT OF HERE TOO WET, TOO COLD

OOOH! LOVELY HOT TEA!

NO GOOD BEING CLEAN IF IT'S COLD

PLENTY OF BLOOMING COLD AT HOME!

WHERE'S SOMEWHERE REALLY HOT? REALLY DRY?

DESERT?

SAHARA? NOTHING THERE — NEVADA?

OF COURSE! LAS VEGAS!

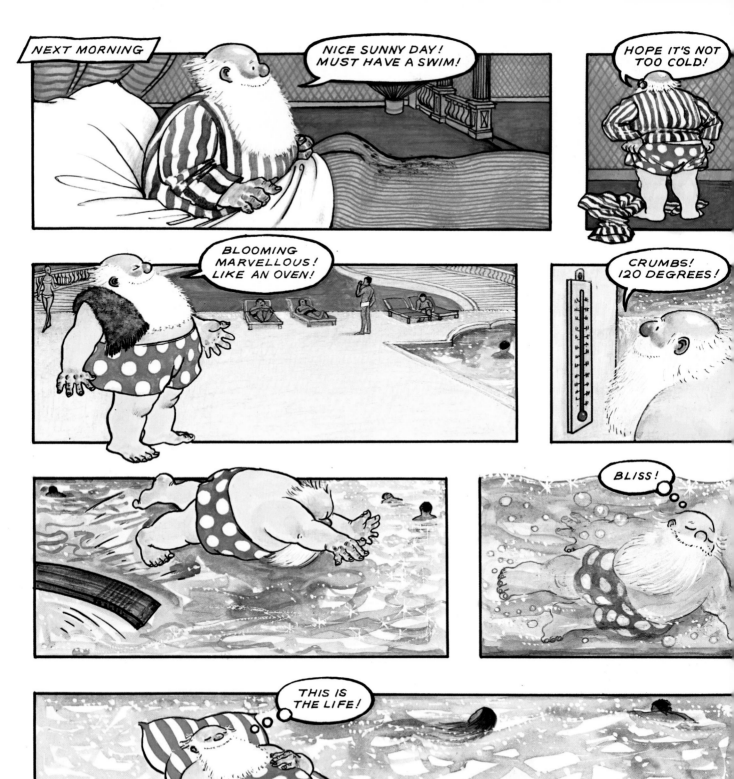

SO THE LAZY DAYS AND WICKED NIGHTS FLY BY, UNTIL........

NEXT MORNING

THANK HEAVEN THAT'S OVER

BETTER GET THE CAT AND DOG

HULLO CAT! HULLO DOG!

THERE'S THE BLOOMING POST ALREADY

GETS EARLIER EVERY BLOOMING YEAR

BETTER GET DOWN TO IT IN A MINUTE

GET ME TUM BACK TO NORMAL

The End